SONGS OF A DEAD FOREST

TRAVIS WADE BEATY

Published by Water Dragon Publishing
waterdragonpublishing.com

An imprint of Paper Angel Press
paperangelpress.com

ISBN 978-1-957146-67-6 (Trade Paperback)

FIRST EDITION

10 9 8 7 6 5 4 3 2 1

SONGS OF A
DEAD FOREST

NEVER IN PETH'S LIFE had her roots come out of their own accord. Nor had she ever seen it happen to another dryad. Such a thing happened in goblin-tales to willful youths who strayed too far from their home forests, wicked little saplings who disobeyed their elders and so found themselves stuck in some nightmarish desert. She had always known it was possible, of course, but could only occur if a dryad had done something extremely stupid — or desperate.

"Curse the wind," Peth muttered.

Her roots had crept out of the soles of her feet as she slept. Now they stuck her to the earth. She pulled herself free, but not before losing her balance and falling flat on her back. She stared up at the dawn sky through the black trees of this strange, dying forest and let darkness cover her heart.

For weeks, she had told herself she still journeyed under the watch of Autumn, but now she could no longer deny Winter's reign. Its cold winds pierced her bark and chilled her bones, commanding her to root down, to sleep until Spring returned. She blasphemed against the Seasons with each step north, but to halt her journey meant death. Worse, it meant failing her grandmother.

It had been little over half a year since Grandy Wik had gripped Peth's hand and spoken her last words, but it felt like a lifetime.

"Go north," Grandy had commanded, "Take my ashes to Greentide, the forest of my birth. Promise me. Swear it!"

Peth had sworn it. She burned Grandy Wik's gnarled and withered body, poured her ashes into a tightly woven pouch coated in bee's wax, and left behind the desolate remains of her home forest. Spring had only just begun then. Peth thought she'd have plenty of time.

But the way north had changed. Grandy described a trek full of forests and prairies. Peth found mostly plains of dull green grass. And the further Peth made her way north, the less of Grandy's directions made any sense. The Fellians and their foul fungus had altered the terrain beyond comprehension.

The red web had come over the mountains along with The Fellians, crammed in the ruts of their cartwheels, clinging to the hems of their robes, nestled in the hides of their livestock. Its spores flew up on the careless winds and gently spread their doom over a country dryads had tended ever since Iwish, daughter of the sea, had leapt out of the ocean with her basket full of acorns. Its crimson threads spread under the earth, suffocating the roots of most trees, shrubs, and flowers. No digging, cutting, or burning away could stop it. A century later, the great dryad warriors who had fought back the initial Fellian invasion, who had inspired so many songs of triumph, had all sunk into the great unknowable depths of the earth. And Peth, the only dryad born of the Darkwood in all that time, journeyed alone across a ruined landscape.

A sparrow landed on Peth's head and chirped its demands. Peth ignored the bird and began scraping the roots from the soles of her feet with a small flat stone. The sparrow danced around her, chirping, hopping, insisting.

Grandy Wik's stern, yet wispy voice came into Peth's head.

"*The Lament of Iwish* must begin with a wail. It must come from the gut and the back of the throat."

Peth picked at the bare and brittle tangle of branches protruding from the crown of her head and scowled at the sparrow. "Our songs are dead. I will not resurrect them so a lump of feathers can flap their wings and squawk for more. Shoo!"

She made to swipe at the bird, but stopped as she sensed a queer vibration beneath her feet. She closed her eyes and pressed a palm against the earth. Pushing past the strain of the red web, she felt a quiver of sorcery snaking through the soil.

It whispered. *I will find you.*

Peth cursed and spat. Was it not enough to watch the dryads die out from afar? Now these men came to hunt the last of her kind?

Perhaps she could stand her ground. She'd shake hands with the flames of her fire and let them set her whole tired body aflame. Her senses would heighten. Her strength would double. No sorcerer could stand against a blazing dryad.

But how long would her blaze last? How long before the fire burned past her bark and devoured the tender fibers beneath? And even if she managed to put the flames out after vanquishing her foes, her body, so exhausted, would surrender to her roots. The red web would have her.

"I have ashes to deliver," she said, scolding the sparrow as if the whole thing had been its idea.

She kicked dirt over the flames, the bird flew off, and Peth ran from the sorcery, with the swiftest, lightest steps her aching joints would allow. But no matter how Peth wove herself through the trees, the magic followed.

Stop running. Come now. All will be forgiven.

She halted when she came to a large clearing where pale ash covered the forest floor. Here lay yet another dryad grave, where all the keepers of this forest had been reunited with the soil in one final blaze.

A green blur rushed through the clearing, kicking up a trail of ash behind until it disappeared into the trees as fast as it had come. Peth thought she had seen —

"Seasons save me," she whispered. "I've gone mad."

Magic swelled around her until she could taste it in the air: a mix of burning metal and carrion. A Fellian floated out of the trees wearing a long white beard and a billowing silver robe. In each hand, he held an oblong rust-colored stone. He frowned at Peth and lowered his hovering form to the ground.

"Where is the child?"

Peth couldn't respond. Having not seen another soul in months, she pondered whether this pale apparition was nothing more than some forest spirit playing with her mind.

"Urah, you old fool," a cool, high voice called from behind. "You're in for it now."

Peth turned to see the youngest and oddest dryad she had ever laid eyes on. The sapling's mantis green skin held not a speck of bark. Instead of moss, she wore tightly coiled ivy vines that mimicked a Fellian tunic. And where her head branches ought to have been, there was nothing but a smooth bald head.

"Mer, don't be foolish," Urah said. "Come now."

"Or what?" Mer said. She stood in a low crouch, her casting stone at the ready. "Will you fight this wild dryad? She told me she's ready to blaze. She called her kin, you know. They'll be here soon."

The sorcerer laughed. "Look at her bark, Mer. She's not from this forest. She's clearly from the south." He cocked his head at Peth. "What are you doing up here, old troll? Looking for Greentide like this little imp? It's a fool's errand. Greentide has fallen to the red web, just like all the rest."

"That's a lie!" Mer yelled.

"Watch your tone, young lady."

The sorcerer murmured an incantation and gestured with one of his stones. It released a puff of smoke and Mer cried out as an invisible force pulled her to the ground. She flailed across the ash toward the sorcerer and the palpable fear in her eyes snapped Peth out of her stupor. She reached down and caught Mer under one arm. The sorcerer's sickening magic pulsed up her shoulder and into the base of her skull. She gritted her teeth and held firm as her stomach tied itself in a knot. Cursing, Urah pulled down his stone and, much to Peth's relief, the magic fell away.

"Get him!" Mer shouted. "Now!"

If the sorcerer cast another spell, Peth would certainly vomit or pass out, maybe both, but she couldn't let him know that. She shook her head to clear her vision and met Urah's gaze.

"You have desecrated this forest with your sorcery," she said. "Leave now before it demands recompense!"

"This forest," Urah said, "Will do nothing but slowly die like all the rest. Listen, troll, you are confused. I understand this child looks like one of yours, but I assure you she is not. She was raised in a Fellian city and is considered a child of Lord Augurian."

"Liar," Mer shouted, coming to her feet. "I was stolen!"

Urah swirled his stones and spat out an incantation. Peth flinched, but nothing came her way.

"You do not wish to meet the creatures I have summoned," Urah said. "I'm not playing games anymore. I will cancel the spell, but only if you come now. There's no need to suffer."

Mer whispered at Peth through her teeth. "Hold still. I'll set you ablaze." With a single word spoken, she shot a burst of flame from her stone.

"No!" Peth shouted. "Stop!"

She smacked the stone out of Mer's hand. The flame went out. The stone rolled into the ash, and Mer dove after it.

With a chuckle, Urah waved a hand. A dark buzzing cloud swooped around him. Peth had a moment to recognize a wood-fly swarm before it rushed at her. She dropped to the ground and rolled in the ash in a desperate attempt to shake them off. It would only take them a few minutes to chew through her bark and begin devouring her from the inside out. Mer, who had retrieved her casting stone, swung her arms in large swooping arcs. She sent blasts of light at the oncoming flies, but they barely did any good. The swarm swooped around the spells and continued their assault.

Peth stopped rolling and put her palms to the ground. She beseeched the forest for help. The strangled mesh of roots beneath the earth gave out a meager groan. She heard Grandy Wik's voice in her head.

"The Lament of Iwish ..."

But Peth would not sing dead songs. Could not sing them. She searched the ash until her hand gripped a good-sized rock and hurled it at the sorcerer's head. He dodged the throw, but the distraction allowed Mer to hit him full-on with one of her blasts of light. He fell flat onto his back. Peth thanked the Seasons and ran into the trees.

She sprinted for the nearby river and, holding Grandy's ashes over her head, plunged in. The wood-flies infesting her bark stopped their frenzied chewing as they drowned in the icy water. A moment later, Mer burst from the tree line and dove in.

"Where is the sorcerer?" Peth shouted.

Mer gave no response and swam past, gliding downstream, easy as an eel. Peth followed her, paddling awkwardly as she used one hand to hold Grandy's ashes above the water.

She caught sight of a log floating nearby and grabbed hold of it.

"Here," she shouted when she caught up to Mer. "We ought to let the river take us."

Mer scowled from the other side of the log, but reach out and held tight.

•　　•　　•

When the sun began to sink beneath the horizon, Peth let go of the log and grabbed Mer's shoulder. They climbed onto the river bank and Peth watched in wonder as Mer cast a spell that evaporated all the water from her body. She pointed her casting stone at Peth next, but Peth waved her off.

"None of that," she said. "I'm fine."

Delirious and exhausted, she fell onto her back in the wet earth.

"What are you doing?" Mer asked.

"Sleeping."

"Not down here. You'll be covered in waterbugs and heaven only knows what else in the morning."

"A good breakfast."

"Blech. Up! We'll camp atop the river bank."

Peth ignored the sapling. A rock smacked her arm.

"Wake up!" Mer yelled. "We're not sleeping down here!"

Peth didn't budge. Another rock struck her leg and another — this one significantly sharper than the others.

She sprang up and bounded at the young dryad. Mer held her casting stone out and cowered, her eyes wide with terror. Peth froze, surprised by her own anger.

"Easy, child," she said. "I just happen to be one of those odd dryads that don't like to be pelted with rocks."

Mer took another step back. "And what kind of dryad are you?"

"A tired one. Old and tired. That's all." She sat down in the mud and put her head between her knees.

"Oh," Mer said. "You're a coward."

"What?"

"Look at you. All that hard bark gone to waste. A dryad of Greentide would never have run from an old man like that."

"Greentide?" Peth said. "Is that where you're from?"

"That's right. I was stolen and now I'm heading back."

"Are there more dryads? At Greentide?"

Mer scowled. "Aye, and if you harm me, they'll stomp you into wood chips."

Peth shook her head. Dare she hope?

"My name is Peth. I was born of the Darkwood, which is no more, but once stood many hills and valleys south of here. Until this morning, I thought I might be the last dryad in all the world. This morning I thought I might be going mad. Perhaps I have gone mad. That's something I would do. Dream up a little imp to throw rocks at me."

"Gods," Mer said, "You've gone buggy!"

"I won't hurt you, child. Whether you be a dream or not. I swear it by the Darkwood."

"I'm not a child," Mer said. "And I'm not a dream. And what good is it to swear by a dead forest?"

Peth grimaced. The faces of her many grandmothers rushed into her head. She bit her lip to keep the tears back.

Mer stared at her feet and rubbed her smooth head.

"We could have beaten him," she said.

She marched up the river bank to the tall reeds above and stomped around until she'd flattened out a portion. She plopped down and waved her stone through the air, conjuring a yellow ball of light that hovered low to the ground.

"A good beacon for the sorcerer," Peth called out.

"I put a cloaking spell over it. I'm not stupid."

Peth, deciding it was best if they stuck together, crawled up the river bank. Up close, the sapling's face glowed golden in the spell's unnatural light. The sight made Peth uneasy. A barkless dryad without head branches looked disturbingly human.

"If you grew out your bark, you would find the mud by the river quite nice. And you wouldn't need to waste your stone on spells for warmth."

"Seeing as I'm not growing bark in the next minute, I'm going to use this spell. Any other advice?"

Peth shook her head. She sat a tolerable distance from Mer's magic, checked her pouch, saw that Grandy's ashes were dry, and thanked the Seasons.

"Are you going to be fussy about my spells?" Mer asked.

"Men's magic is a blasphemy. A mockery of the Seasons. I was raised —"

"I don't need a lecture. I hate Fellian sorcery more than anyone. But I was raised on these spells. I can't just give them up. Save your scorn."

"I'll keep my scorn if you keep from throwing rocks."

"Go to sleep already. If the old man finds us, I'll be sure to wake you so you can *not* fight him and we can run away like scared little mice again."

•　　•　　•

In the morning, Peth found herself once more stuck in the earth. How in all the green earth had she forgotten about her roots? Her heart raced as she yanked at her ankles to no avail. She squatted and rocked back and forth until, nearly in tears, she fell over, her feet pulling up clods of dirt along with her roots. She hobbled over to scrape the soles of her feet clean on a piece of granite jutting out from the river bank. When she finished, she turned to see Mer watching. The impossibly green sapling sat cross-legged in the grass, rolling her casting stone between the palms of her hands.

"What's wrong with your feet?"

"Nothing," Peth said. She retrieved her pouch and slung it over her shoulder.

"Nothing?" Mer asked.

Peth ignored her and surveyed the landscape.

The river rushed ever north until it disappeared over the long line of the horizon. The grassy plains stretched out on either side as far as the eye could see, its pale green surface rippling with the wind. Mean-looking clouds flew in from the east.

"You're rooting down," Mer said. "You won't make it but a few days."

"If you knew what was wrong, why did you ask?"

"To see if I could get a straight answer. It appears not. In *The Book of Thil*, does it not say, 'The Seasons scorn deceiving hearts.'"

Peth grunted. "Books? We had no books in the Darkwood. We ought to be moving."

Peth peered into her pouch to be sure Grandy's ashes were safe and began walking north, alongside the river.

"You don't know the story of Thil?" Mer asked, jogging to keep pace with Peth's long stride.

"I know more than the story. I know the song. That was my calling in the Darkwood. I was a poet. Sorry to disappoint, but I'm no warrior hero like Thil, ready to crush all my foes in a storm of fist and fire."

"When Urah finds us, we'll have to fight. If I'm not returned, Lord Augurian will have his head. He can't go back without me. Gods! His face when he saw you! And then I had him on his back and you fled. You ran. Right when we had him!"

"You're forgetting the wood-flies."

"I would have handled the flies if you had gone after the old man."

Peth shook her head. "You're from Greentide, yes? So you know the way?"

Mer stopped and rubbed her head. "I was taken when I was very young. I only know it's north. The river will guide us, yes?"

"If it is the right river. I lost my way weeks ago. I know this is either the Shone or the Durthle. I haven't a clue which."

One of Peth's roots caught in the soil and she stumbled. Cursing, she knelt to scrape her feet clean yet again.

Mer pulled out her casting stone. "Hold still."

"No!" Peth cried.

"This will keep the moisture in your fibers. It's what I use on myself. It won't hurt."

"It's poison. Worse than poison! I won't have that corruption under my bark. Understood?"

Mer frowned and shook her head. "You won't make it."

"You're an odd one," Peth said. "Quoting *The Song of Thil* one moment and the next you care nothing for the will of the Seasons. We'll stay near the water. If I wet my feet in the river now and then, I'll be fine as flowers. Try to keep up."

A cold rain fell and they had to walk against the wind. Peth had many questions for the young dryad, but couldn't bring herself to ask any. She feared Mer would ask her own questions in return, and Peth couldn't bear to speak of her past. Soon, though, the wind rushed over the plains in such great gales that it was impossible to speak and be heard.

Around mid-day, the wind and rain let up. The heavy grey-green clouds gave way to a bright gold and violet sky, dappled with fluffs of white.

A raven swooped out of the sky and landed on Peth's head branches. "Song," it croaked.

When Peth swat at it, the bird flitted over to perch on Mer's outstretched hand.

"There are no songs here," Peth said. "Can you guide us to Greentide? There will be a great many songs if we find dryads there."

"Song," The bird repeated.

Mer cleared her throat and sang the opening lines to an old quarryman's folk song. The raven squawked and flapped its wings.

"Tree-tree," the bird said. "Tree song."

Mer looked to Peth.

"No," Peth said.

The raven cocked its head and flew off.

"Wait," Mer yelled, "Greentide! How far are we from Greentide?"

The bird flew on.

"Are there bugs in your brain?" Mer asked. "All it wanted was a song."

"Greentide is north," Peth said. "The river will guide us."

When night set in, they found a cluster of large granite boulders next to the river and sat among them to shield themselves from the chill winds. Peth lifted one of the boulders and found a slew of insects to dine on. Mer had no qualms with the fare and the two munched in silence. Peth made sure to set her feet on a small boulder to keep her roots from the soil and closed her eyes.

"We're being hunted," Mer said. "We're hardly making progress because you have to scrape your feet clean every other hour. All it wanted was a song."

"What do I owe a bird?"

Mer snorted. "If she could guide us to Greentide, I would say you'd owe a bird everything."

"My songs belong to the Darkwood. No one else. And I have sung for the birds plenty. When the last of my kin died, I sang every song. The birds came. They sat in the dead limbs of the Darkwood and watched in silence. I was glad to see them. Happy to have someone to share ..."

Peth gritted her teeth until her eyes dried.

"When I was done. When I had no more tears left in me and my throat was raw from singing, what did all those birds do? They flew off. Left me to find some new amusement. So, yes, I have sung enough for the birds."

Mer said no more.

When Peth finally fell asleep, she dreamt she was still a green-skinned sapling, standing straight as a reed before Grandy Wik.

"Stop that sound," Grandy scolded. "Sing from your core. Sing as if you are the deepest current of The River Shone. You're singing from your head like some mewling bear cub. Start again."

Peth awoke with her stomach in a knot, the air reeking of sorcery.

"Urah!" she thought. "He's found us!"

She rolled over to find Mer waving her casting stone and whispering an incantation. The sickening buzz of magic crawled through Peth's fibers. She vomited until there was nothing left in her stomach and then retched some more. When she was done, she brought herself up to a crouch with a mind to leap at Mer and lay hold of her casting stone. But before she could lunge, she caught sight of her pouch laying upturned. Grandy's ashes had been poured out and were now dancing in the wind.

"What did you do?" she screamed.

"I'm not sorry," Mer said. "I had to keep you from rooting down. It's the only way you'll make it."

"I mean this!" Peth held up the pouch.

"Thought you might have some weapon in there. The way you were clutching at it."

A gust of wind blew away what remained of the ashes. Grandy's final wish, the oath Peth had sworn, the months of hard travel, all this blaspheming against Winter — all vanished.

She turned back to the sapling and set her eyes on the casting stone. Mer's face went pale. She cast a spell that surrounded her with a translucent shell of blue light.

Peth ran up and punched the shield. A jolt of what felt like a small bolt of lightning ran up her arm. She shook her hand out and tried again, this time placing her palm firmly against the surface of the shield and pressing hard. Its blue light flickered. She put her full weight behind it.

Her hand began to slide through the shield. The magic constricted around her arm. Its pressure felt almost unbearable, but she pressed on until her whole arm passed through. She tore the stone from Mer's hand, and the shield blinked out.

"No!" Mer screamed.

Peth threw the stone as far as she could. It became a speck against the pale morning sky and vanished.

Mer threw herself at Peth, punching and kicking. With a swipe of her arm, Peth sent the sapling rolling across the grass.

"Troll!," Mer screamed. "Do you know how hard it is to find omarite? Now I can't cast anything. If he finds us, we're done for."

"Us? You mean if he finds *you*." Peth shook her limbs as if she could somehow shake off the corruption still writhing under her skin. "Seasons save me, she's a Fellian! A Fellian! That's what she is!"

"Who are you talking to, you crazy old log? *I'm* not a dryad? You don't even have a forest."

She flung a patch of grass at Peth. "Go! Leave. I'd hate to show up to Greentide with a cowardly sack of firewood like you. Go on! Root down in the middle of nowhere. I hope Urah finds you and carves you into a paperweight!"

Peth held up her empty pouch. "That was the ashes of my dearest grandmother you laid out. The one thing I had left of my home forest. You have desecrated not only my body, but my ancestors."

Mer's lip trembled.

"How was I supposed to know that? Go! Get out of here!"

Peth tried to walk away with dignity, but had to pick up her pace when Mer switched from clods of grass to rocks.

She jogged all day along the river, certain Mer was following at a distance, but when the sun hung low and red over the horizon, there was no sign of the sapling.

"Right as rain," Peth thought. "She has come to her senses and gone back to the sorcerer."

She sat on the river bank and watched as the water shifted from deep blue to indigo, to black shimmering with pale moonlight. She tried to doze off, but every little rustle of wind made her sit up and search the dark for the sapling. She rubbed her feet and gasped at the smoothness of her soles. Her roots had not troubled her all day. Mer's spell had worked.

"Seasons forgive," she whispered.

She looked over the river, to the endless black of night beyond. She imagined a pine tree standing tall, and another, and another. She inhaled and tried to conjure the scent of sea air as Grandy had described it: deep green seaweed mingled with pine, briny fish, and just a pinch of sulfur. She imagined tall, slender dryads striding out of the trees, their head branches full of dark green leaves. They waved at Peth. She waved back.

"Where is the other one?" They asked.

"There is only me," she said. "The other one, she was not …"

Greentide melted back into darkness.

"She was a Fellian. I can't turn back. I have ashes to deliver."

She grasped the pouch around her waist and felt how light it had become. Her stomach sank. She picked at her head branches and thought of how the sapling had the same nervous habit, only Mer had nothing to pick at. But she probably did have head-branches once, didn't she? Little green twigs someone had shorn off to make her look more like themselves. Peth closed her eyes and saw the sorcerer's thin smile, the sparkle in his eye when he'd thrown those wood-flies.

Peth stood and began walking back the way she'd come. It was not long before she sensed Urah's death-tainted magic and broke into a sprint. She followed it to the place where she and Mer had camped the night before. The mud and grass had been trampled by many feet as if a great struggle had taken place. Peth put her palms to the ground and focused until she could distinguish Mer's magic from the sorcerer's. She followed the faint vibrations until they led to Mer's casting stone sitting in the grass, nearly covered in the fat snowflakes which had begun to fall.

"Winter, forgive me," Peth said. "I am coming."

•   •   •

She saw the sorcerer's fire first, flickering through the snow. She dropped to the ground and crawled through the ankle-deep snow to the crest of a small hill. Urah sat huddled by his fire, his silver robe whipping in the wind. Other figures sat by another fire twenty paces away — four men, huddled close. Peth guessed by their simple dress that they were not soldiers, but nearby quarrymen, paid a handsome fee by the sorcerer. Shame swept over Peth as she realized Urah had hired the men thinking he'd have to go through a full-grown dryad to get at the sapling.

Mer sat between the two fires with her back against a tall post that had been driven into the ground, her hands tied behind it.

The sun rose, turning the world from hazy grey to dazzling white. The snow came down harder. The wind picked up. Peth rubbed her hands together for warmth and noticed little wispy roots sprouting from the back of her hands. She looked herself over and saw the same growing from her shins and even her thighs. Mer's magic had worn off and Winter now laid claim two-fold.

Urah rose from his fire and ducked into his silver canvas tent. The men turned their backs to Peth, trying to shield themselves from the wind. She wouldn't get a better chance.

Peth began to shake all over, but not from the cold. "Grandy," she whispered. "I'm scared."

"*The Lament of Iwish*," Grandy said, "begins with a wail."

"Yes," Peth whispered. "I will join you soon, Grandy. And we will sing all the songs."

She crawled on her belly through the snow for as long as she could without being seen. One of the men stood when she was fifty paces away. Two pulled up crossbows when she came to her feet. They fired their weapons when she broke into a sprint. She punched one in the jaw and threw another into the snow. Both men scrambled to their feet and fled. Of the two men left, one shot an arrow before running off, and the other went for the campfire. Peth pulled the arrow from her chest. It felt like a wasp's sting from when she had been young and her bark had not yet fully grown in. The man who went for the fire pulled out a long flaming log and held it like a weapon. He clearly knew very little about dryads.

Peth lunged for the fire, but it fizzled out before she could touch it. The air filled with the deathly stench of Urah's magic. The man threw the log down and joined his fellow quarrymen in their mad dash over the snowy plains.

Peth turned to face the sorcerer. He waved his smoking red stones and the flames went out in both fire pits. Peth ran at him and nearly closed the distance before Urah sent out a great wave of magic that wrapped itself tightly around Peth's body, freezing her in mid-step. She strained, but could only manage to look out the corner of her eye and see Mer on the ground, gagged with a handkerchief, staring wide-eyed at the scene.

"Why must you devils be so hard to kill?" Urah yelled. "Can't set you on fire. Can't cut through your bark. But you have lungs, don't you?"

He moved his stones askew and bared his teeth. The magic around Peth tightened until she could no longer draw breath.

So this was it. The end of her failed journey. She let tears fall from her eyes and took a perverse joy in knowing Urah could not stop her weeping. She groaned deep in her gut, only now realizing how much sorrow she had locked away. It welled up in her chest and, with nowhere to go, shuddered through her body. Her throat opened for an instant and she released a short, pained cry.

"There's your wail, Grandy," she thought.

She put the first notes of *The Lament of Iwish* into her strained voice. Her songs were not dead. Not quite. The last of the Darkwood lived yet and her song would be sung to the end.

Half a mile away, the quarrymen, still fleeing, heard the wail and came to halt. For a moment, they couldn't move, so strong was their urge to hear that haunting voice again. From the opposite direction of the wail, they beheld a strange sight. A black cloud darted through the snow. As it sped over their heads, they heard it calling out in many voices, "Song, song, song."

Urah jerked his stones down and let out a roar. His magic tightened until it became a fist clenched at Peth's throat. As the edges of her vision darkened, she saw a little black figure flutter out of the snow and land on Urah's head.

"Song," it croaked.

Urah swatted at the bird, but as he did, a whole flock of ravens fell on him.

"Song" they all croaked. "Song, song, song."

Urah fell under a dark shroud of beak and wing. The magic gripping Peth fell away. She collapsed, but continued singing as she scrambled to Mer and untied her.

Once Mer was free, Peth pulled the casting stone from her pouch and smacked it into the sapling's hand.

"Fire! Now!"

Mer clamped her eyes shut and slashed her stone through the air. Peth reached for the flames that flew out and watched as they took hold of her bark and crackled up her arm.

"More!" She yelled.

Mer cast her fire again and again. The fire soon swept over Peth's face and, for a moment, she was blinded by the light. Searing heat enveloped her and the next moment all her pain was gone. She was ablaze. Her mind hummed and every fiber in her being felt as if it could tear the sun out of the sky.

The frantic, murderous pile of ravens exploded like the splinters of an ancient oak struck through with lightning. Urah emerged from their center covered in blood. He sent up blasts of white light, and the ravens, like leaves on the wind, disappeared into the snow-filled sky. The sorcerer turned his gaze upon Peth, his eyes shining like polished bone amid a bloodstained face. Peth ran at him, her heart swelling in her chest, the sorrowful melody of *The Lament of Iwish* pouring from her mouth.

Urah swung his stones wildly, screaming incantations. He sent thundering pulses of magic, but nothing could hold back the last of the Darkwood. When she wrenched the casting stones from Urah, his hands slipped free of her grasp and he fled.

She made to follow him, to crush his bones into dust, but her skin began to sting. The fire had burned past her bark. The sting blossomed into an all-encompassing pain. She screamed and fell to the ground. With what little mind she had left, she rolled through the snow to put out the flames.

As soon as she was free from the fire, fresh roots sprang from not only her feet, but her hands and knees — from any part of her touching the soil. She knew there was no fighting it now. Her joints stiffened. Her eyes sealed shut. Her roots delved deep into the earth.

•　　•　　•

Peth searched the soil as if she might find the familiar embrace of the Darkwood, as if all her grandmothers might join in, bind their roots to hers, and sing gentle songs until Spring returned. But Peth found only a vast empty darkness.

Still, her roots searched, unable to stop their yearning to connect, to bind, to meld into a forest, until, at last, Peth heard a faint voice whispering through the soil.

"You sang it well, child."

"Grandmother, I lost your ashes."

"I was afraid you had lost our songs. That these harsh winds had swept them from your heart."

"What does it matter? I have failed."

"What do my ashes matter? I only wanted you to go, child. How many times did I tell you to go and seek out other dryads? But you would not leave our home which had become nothing but a place of death."

"Grandy, I couldn't —"

"Shush! There's no time for that. Forget my ashes. Remember me. Remember my love, you beautiful child of the Darkwood. Up you go. Hurry!"

Something dark, hungry, and red reached out for Peth, but it was too late.

•　　　•　　　•

Peth itched all over as if awakening to the first warm rain of Spring. She pulled up a hand and felt the roots holding her to the earth give way. Wiping the black soot from her arms, she revealed the clay color of her barkless skin beneath. Everything came back to her. She had rooted down. She had blazed. She had run at the sorcerer.

"Urah," she said, her voice cracked and thin.

"Easy, big oak," Mer said. The sapling looked pale and tired. "The old man is gone. The ravens finished what you started. They left him to rot out there. Something came in the night and drug the remains away. I didn't care to find out what it was."

Peth took a step forward. She felt light-headed, but also strong. Her fibers itched to move, to run. And she felt a crawling sensation under her skin, one she found unexpectedly tolerable.

"Forgive me," Mer said. "For pumping you full of magic, but I couldn't just leave you."

"It is Winter we must ask forgiveness from," Peth said. She stared at the wet, snowless grass. It squished under her feet. "Why does it feel like Spring? How long have I been rooted down?"

"You've been stuck there two days," Mer said. "I had to cast my spells day and night to bring you back. Nearly burned half my stone away. Not to worry, we have Urah's stones now. It didn't hurt that the weather took a turn. The last of the snow melted this morning. It's as if Spring came early. I hope it lasts."

A raven flew down and perched on Mer's arm. "Song," the bird croaked.

"Please sing to them," Mer said. "They won't shut up about it."

Peth met the blank gaze of the raven. "Greentide," she said.

"Song."

Peth thumped one hand against her chest in a steady rhythm and began *The Song of the Darkwood*. The raven flew up to dip and weave through the sky.

"You think they'll lead us to Greentide?" Mer asked.

"Maybe," Peth said. "I don't know. But we'll follow them."

Mer burst into tears. "I lied. I don't know where I'm from. All I know of Greentide is what I've read in books. I barely remember my home forest."

Peth put a hand on the sapling's shoulder.

"There's a song we learn in the Darkwood as our first. Would you like me to teach it to you?"

Mer wiped her eyes and shook her head. "No. I can't. I can't sing like you."

"It begins quiet," Peth said. "With a whisper. You must sing it as if you are a seed waiting patient in the earth."

The two dryads sang a gentle melody of green things, of birth and renewal. The ravens flew north in rhythm with their song. The dryads followed.

ABOUT THE AUTHOR

Travis Wade Beaty has been a professional actor, Spider-Man at children's birthday parties, an inventory specialist of fine and rare wine, and a teacher, but his favorite job by far is being a stay-at-home dad to twin girls, two cats, and a dog.

His stories have appeared in Zombies Need Brains' *NOIR* anthology, *Metaphorosis Magazine*, *Metastellar*, and elsewhere. Travis grew up in Indiana, and after spending a good deal of his twenties in Los Angeles, now resides in Washington, DC.

YOU MIGHT ALSO ENJOY

THE ALCHEMIST DAUGHTER

by Paul S. Moore

When a concoction of ethers channels a little of their magic properties to one location, inspiration springs to life.

GREY MOTHER MOUNTAIN

by Elyse Russell

When her village is destroyed, an elderly woman seeks help from the last remaining dragon to get revenge.

POSSESSION IS NINE-TENTHS

by J Dark

Possession might be 9/10th of the law. But no one mentioned 9/10th of what.

Available in digital and trade paperback editions from
Water Dragon Publishing
waterdragonpublishing.com